r Te'

'48°

How Bear Lost His Tail

by Mick Gowar and Andy Catling

FRANKLIN WATTS
LONDON • SYDNEY

Chapter 1

It was winter in the ice-cold North.

The ground was hard. The trees in the forest

were covered with snow. It was so cold

that even the rivers had frozen.

Otter hadn't caught any fish for days and days.

She and her children were very hungry.

"Today I will go down to the sea and fish,"

Otter told her children. "The sea won't be frozen."

When she got to the sea, Otter saw that it was covered with thick ice. But she could see that a hunter had found a way to catch fish.

The hunter had cut a hole in the ice and dropped his fishing line through it. Otter hid and watched as the pile of fish got bigger and bigger.

When the hunter had gone, Otter crept over to the hole.

"I could fish here, too," she said to herself.

Otter dived through the hole and into the freezing sea.

8

Time and time again, she brought a fish back up
through the hole in the ice. Soon there was
a pile of fish to take home to her children.

Chapter 2

Bear was walking along the path from the forest.

He saw Otter, and he saw the big pile of fish.

He walked up to Otter carrying his long, beautiful tail over his arm. Bear was very proud of his long, beautiful tail. He never let it drag on the ground and get dirty.

"What are you doing?" asked Bear.

"Fishing," said Otter.

"Give me your fish," said Bear, rudely. "NOW!"

Bear had a long, beautiful tail, but his manners were terrible.

"I need these fish to feed my children," said Otter.

"Why don't you catch some yourself?"

Bear looked down into the hole.

"How do you catch fish from a hole?" he asked.

"I'm too big to fit in there. Give me your fish."

Otter looked at Bear's long, beautiful tail and

she had an idea. She would play a trick on Bear.

Then she could keep all the fish she had caught

for her children.

"I catch fish with my tail," said Otter.

"How?" asked Bear.

16

"I put my tail in the hole and wiggle it from side to side," said Otter. "Then I wait. The fish think my tail is something good to eat, and grab it. When I feel a fish nibble, I pull out my tail and there's a delicious fish on the end!'

Bear frowned. "Won't the fish hurt my tail?"
he asked.

Otter showed her tail to Bear. "There's not
a mark on my tail," she said, "and with
your long tail, you're sure to catch lots of fish.
You just need to wait long enough."

Now, Bear had a long, beautiful tail, but he was very silly. Slowly, he lowered his tail into the hole. Otter smiled to herself, picked up her fish and went home.

Chapter 3

Bear wiggled his tail in the cold water

and waited. There wasn't a nibble.

He wiggled his tail some more.

There wasn't a bite.

He wiggled his tail harder and waited again.

He waited for a whole hour.

Bear was getting colder and so was his tail.

Bear kept on wiggling and waiting,

hour after hour after hour,

just as Otter had told him to.

After he had been there for a long time,

his tail wouldn't move.

He tried to wiggle it again,

but it still wouldn't move.

Bear tried to stand up, but he couldn't move at all.
The hole in the ice had frozen over and his tail
was stuck in the ice as tight as a stick in a lolly.

"Help!" shouted Bear. "I'm stuck in the ice!"

All the animals and people were in their homes,

keeping as warm as they could. No one heard

Bear and no one came to help him.

Bear pulled and pulled, but his tail was stuck fast.

Bear pulled harder and harder until …

SNAP!

"NO!" yelled Bear. He wasn't stuck anymore,

but something was wrong.

"Where is my long, beautiful tail?" yelled Bear.

His tail was stuck in the ice and all he had left

was a small, brown stump.

Bear shuffled sadly home.
He soaked his small, brown
stump in warm water,

he rubbed it
with ointment,

he even tried

stretching it.

28

But nothing made his tail grow.

Bear had lost his long, beautiful tail.

And from that day on, all bears have just

a small, brown stump where there was once

a long, beautiful tail.

Things to think about

1. How can you tell that Otter is clever?
2. Why does Otter want to trick Bear?
3. Do you think that Bear should have believed Otter so easily?
4. What do you think the message of this story might be?
5. Can you think of any other stories which tell us why animals look the way they do?

Write it yourself

This traditional tale tries to explain why bears have a short, stumpy tail. Try to write your own story explaining why an animal looks the way it does.

Plan your story before you begin to write it.
Start off with a story map:
• a beginning to introduce the characters and where your story is set (the setting);
• a problem which the main characters will need to fix in the story;
• an ending where the problems are resolved.

Get writing! Try to use interesting noun phrases such as "ice-cold North" to describe your story world and excite your reader.

Notes for parents and carers

Independent reading

This series is designed to provide an opportunity for your child to read independently, for pleasure and enjoyment. These notes are written for you to help your child make the most of this book.

About the book

This retelling of a Native American traditional tale explains how Bear comes to have his short, stumpy tail. It also sends a strong message about not believing everything you are told! Bear's vanity about his tail and his attempt to bully Otter out of her fish lead him to losing his tail forever.

Before reading

Ask your child why they have selected this book. Look at the title and blurb together. What do they think it will be about? Do they think they will like it?

During reading

Encourage your child to read independently. If they get stuck on a word, remind them that they can sound it out in syllable chunks. They can also read on in the sentence and think about what would make sense.

After reading

Support comprehension and help your child think about the messages in the book that go beyond the story, using the questions on the page opposite.
Give your child a chance to respond to the story, asking:
Did you enjoy the story and why?
Who was your favourite character?
What was your favourite part?
What did you expect to happen at the end?

Franklin Watts
First published in Great Britain in 2018
by The Watts Publishing Group

Copyright © The Watts Publishing Group 2018
All rights reserved.

Series Editors: Jackie Hamley and Melanie Palmer
Series Advisors: Dr Sue Bodman and Glen Franklin
Series Designer: Peter Scoulding

A CIP catalogue record for this book is
available from the British Library.

ISBN 978 1 4451 6285 0 hbk)
ISBN 978 1 4451 6286 7 (pbk)
ISBN 978 1 4451 6284 3 (library ebook)

Printed in China

Franklin Watts
An imprint of
Hachette Children's Group
Part of The Watts Publishing Group
Carmelite House
50 Victoria Embankment
London EC4Y 0DZ

An Hachette UK Company
www.hachette.co.uk

www.franklinwatts.co.uk